THE CASE OF THE
DEAD DUCK

ANNE SCHRAFF

PAGETURNERS

Development and Production: Laurel Associates, Inc.

SADDLEBACK
EDUCATIONAL PUBLISHING
www.sdlback.com

ISBN-13: 978-1-56254-388-4
ISBN-10: 1-56254-388-1
eBook: 978-1-60291-246-5

Printed in the United States of America
15 14 13 12 11 2 3 4 5 6 7

CONTENTS

Chapter 1

Ben Stephens never mentioned his family at the real estate office where he worked. He talked a lot about Kerry Underwood, his steady girlfriend, but he never said a word about his brother, Roy. That was because Roy was on death row in state prison. Ben wasn't about to share something like that. He'd been shamed and horrified when Roy and another guy were arrested. Their crime was a crummy $50 liquor store robbery. But it had ended in the death of a young clerk.

Roy had always been a troublemaker. He'd gotten kicked out of high school in tenth grade and had ended up in a juvenile detention camp when he was 16. Nothing seemed to turn him around. As a young adult, Roy took up with an older criminal named Pulver—and from there things had only gone downhill.

Hardly a day went by that Ben didn't think about that awful night. The young liquor store clerk, Carlos Oliver, had pulled out a gun. He'd managed to get off one shot, mortally wounding Pulver. But at the same moment, Oliver had taken a slug to the forehead that had eventually killed him. Before Pulver had died, he'd told the police that Ben's brother Roy had fired the shot that killed the liquor store clerk.

Roy Stephens had hidden out for a week before the police cornered him. Of course he had denied being the gunman at the liquor store that night. He denied being there at all. But why *wouldn't* he deny it? He was looking at a murder rap. But after a very quick trial, Roy Stephens had been convicted of first-degree murder and sentenced to death. It didn't seem real. The horror of it all was still hard for Ben to believe.

"Hey, Ben," one of the other real estate agents called out, "there's a couple coming over to look at that house on Auburn. Can you handle it?"

"Sure thing," Ben said. He was the youngest agent in the office, but he was doing pretty well. He was a personable guy who worked very hard to match buyers and sellers. Because he was new, he didn't get the choice listings. But he did very well with those he got—like that house over on Auburn. It was in a rundown neighborhood. Only a young couple without much money for a down payment would want to buy it.

Ben pulled out a fact sheet about the listing and waited for the clients to arrive. While he waited, his thoughts drifted back to his kid brother. Ben was 24, and Roy was two years younger. There was a time—a long, *long* time ago—when they were just two little boys riding their bikes, playing sandlot baseball, and trading baseball cards. Now it took some effort to remember when Roy was that cute, funny little kid, looking up to Ben, trying to imitate him.

There had been so much bad stuff for so many years. Ben remembered the screaming fights between Roy and Mom and Dad. Their parents had made desperate, futile efforts to keep Roy out of trouble. But nothing helped. There were the times he ran away and the times he was busted for drugs. Mom crying, Dad cursing, the shock of the murder charge, and the agony of the trial. Finally—the sentence of death.

Sometimes Ben woke up in a cold sweat in the middle of the night. In one of his nightmares, Roy had escaped from death row. He was standing in Ben's bedroom saying, "I didn't do it, Benny. I swear I didn't. I wasn't even there. No way, man. You gotta hide me. You gotta get me outta this. Benny—remember when the big kids on Illinois Street got after me and you made them back down? You could always fix things for me, Benny. When I got in scrapes, you were there for me every time. *You gotta get me out of this, Benny. I swear I'm innocent.* Don't let them kill me, man."

Ben had awakened in a cold sweat that night, frightened and shaking. But he had never been able to make the nightmares go away.

The young couple arrived at the real estate office. Ben drove them to the house on Auburn in his Mazda.

"We don't have much money to put down," Mr. Gonzales said. "Just what our parents have loaned us."

Mrs. Gonzales was expecting a baby, but she was still working part-time. "We don't expect a big fancy house or anything like that," she said. "It's okay if it's a fixer-upper. Hector is a painter and a mason, and I'm good at sewing curtains and things. We can make a very plain little house look real nice."

9

"Well, this is a nice starter house," Ben said, easily switching into his "friendly real estate agent" mode. "It's been rented for a year or so, and it's not in great shape. You'll see. The place is vacant now and it really needs some tender loving care."

Ben was embarrassed when they pulled up to the small frame house with the weed-choked front lawn. The place looked *awful*. He figured the young couple wouldn't even bother to get out of the car. But they both jumped out and hurried to the front door.

"It's really cute," Mrs. Gonzales said once they were inside. "If this kitchen got a good cleaning and some fresh paint, it would be perfect."

Ben followed them through the rooms, his mind wandering. His brother Roy had a girlfriend at the time the murder was committed. She was a pretty girl named Noreen. Ben liked Noreen. He had even hoped that Noreen would be the one who could finally turn Roy around and get him back on the right path.

Noreen testified at the trial that Roy was with her when the shooting took place. But then she admitted that she was drunk that night. In fact, she claimed that she and Roy were *both* drunk. When she got all her facts mixed up, the jury discounted everything she said. Noreen left the stand sobbing and she never came back.

The voices of the excited young couple discussing the house were like a distant hum in Ben's brain. Again his thoughts had turned to his brother sitting in that cell on death row, waiting for time to run out. Roy's execution probably wouldn't happen for several more years. It seemed like there were always more appeals to exhaust. But eventually it *would* happen. Ben couldn't imagine what it must be like to look ahead to your own execution.

"We want to make a deposit," Mr.

Gonzales said. Ben snapped out of his daze. By the time they left his office an hour later, the deal was done. In all the excitement, Ben had forgotten about his brother's problems. He was thrilled to be basking in the praise of his boss. Now Ben could think of nothing but calling his girlfriend Kerry so they could get together for a little celebration.

But when Ben got home, it all crashed on him again. He hadn't called his parents for a few days—and every time he did call, the conversation was mostly about Roy. It was always so depressing that Ben dreaded calling them. But now he called. He *had* to— especially for his mom's sake. His parents had lost their youngest son. The only son they had left, Ben, owed it to them to be a stand-up guy, and he tried.

"Hi, Mom, how's it going?" he asked.

"Hello, Ben. I'm okay. I went to church today and lit a candle for Roy. Maybe I'm the only person in the world still praying for him, but I'll never stop," Mom said in her sad martyr's voice.

Ben closed his eyes and remembered the parents of the murdered liquor store clerk. They had come to the trial every day. They'd looked at Roy Stephens with pure hatred in their eyes. At the penalty phase of the trial, both parents had taken the stand and sobbed out their grief and bitterness. They'd demanded Roy's life in payment for the loss of their only son. The jury was moved by their grief. It had taken them only four hours to recommend the death penalty.

"Yeah, Mom," Ben said. "Well, keep on praying. You always did your best for Roy. Dad, too."

"I don't know, Ben," she said sadly. "Maybe we didn't. I keep wondering about it. Your father always said I was too easy on Roy. He says I spoiled him, and that's why he went bad. But God knows I never meant to hurt that boy. But how can a mother turn her back on her child—no matter what?" Mom said.

Dad wasn't out there lighting candles for Roy. Ben was sure of that. Dad was angry and bitter. He said that he'd never forgive Roy for bringing such shame on the family, especially his mother—not even after Roy was dead. That's what Dad said. The poor man was so bitter! Sometimes Ben thought that all the trouble they'd had was eating his dad alive. He wouldn't even allow the mention of Roy's name in his house.

"Benny, sometimes I wonder," Mom said forlornly. "Do you ever wonder?"

"About what, Mom?" Ben asked.

"You know—if he did it—if Roy really killed that man. He *swears* that he didn't," Mom said. The poor woman was grasping at straws. Ben figured she must be "in denial," or whatever the psychologists called it.

"The jury was convinced, Mom. They checked Pulver's hands, remember? He hadn't fired a gun, so we know that he didn't shoot the clerk. And he testified that Roy *did*. Why would a dying guy rat out his best friend if it was a lie? Pulver must have known it was truth time, because he *was* dying. And the clerk identified a picture of Roy in the hospital before he died," Ben said.

"But they never found the gun, Benny. You know they never did find the gun. . . . " Mom went on.

"Yeah, they figure he tossed it in a storm drain or something. He'd been hiding out for a week. Why did Roy go into hiding right after the murder? If he really was innocent, he could have come forward immediately. And if he hadn't fired a gun, they would have used scientific evidence to prove that, too," Ben said.

"Oh, but he was scared when he heard what happened! Roy *always* ran and hid when he was scared. You remember that. Benny, a mother should know—shouldn't she? If my boy had

15

done such a terrible thing, wouldn't I *know* it in my heart?"

"I don't think so, Mom. You always gave Roy the benefit of the doubt. But that's okay. It's mother's love, Mom," Ben said, trying to comfort her.

Mom started crying then and said, "I don't know, Benny. I suppose so." Then, with a long deep sigh, she said goodnight and hung up.

Ben slumped down on the sofa. Now he didn't feel much like celebrating the sale of the house on Auburn Street. He pressed his fingertips into his tired eyes.

Was there even a remote possibility that Roy was innocent? Was there the slightest ghost of a chance? Ben sighed and thought of Mom again. Maybe he and Kerry should get married soon. That would be the best thing for Mom— especially when the first baby came: New life to help everyone forget about the end of Roy's life.

Chapter 2

A little while later Ben went over to Kerry's apartment to have some pizza and watch a video. But when the movie was barely underway, Kerry turned to Ben and asked, "What's the matter, honey? I can tell that your mind is a million miles away." When Ben didn't answer her right away, Kerry nodded and sighed, "The usual thing, huh?"

Kerry was the one person Ben had confided in about his grief over Roy. No matter what, she was always patient and understanding. She didn't hold it against Ben that he had a brother awaiting execution on death row.

"Yeah, I'm sorry, Kerry. It just keeps nagging at me. Sometimes I can't help thinking—what if he *didn't* do it?" Ben said. "Or if he *did* do it, why don't they commute his sentence to life?"

Kerry put her arm around Ben's broad shoulders. "Sweetie, think about it. The guy who got killed—that Carlos Oliver—lingered for a week, remember? He identified your brother from the picture they showed him. He said he was absolutely sure that Roy was the guy who shot him, didn't he?"

"Yeah, but so what? A dying guy on heavy medication looks at a snapshot and says 'that's him.' Pulver had this little snapshot of Roy and that's all the cops had to show to the clerk in the hospital. It wasn't even a good picture. What if Pulver hung out with another creep who looked like Roy? I mean—it's not impossible, is it?" Ben asked. But even as he spoke he knew his words were coming out sounding like Mom. He was in denial, too.

"But Ben—Roy and Pulver were *buddies*. If Roy didn't do it, why would

Pulver finger him when he was dying? I've always heard that dying people tell the truth because they've got nothing to lose," Kerry said gently. "It doesn't make sense. Why would Pulver lie like that?"

"I don't know," Ben admitted. "He was a creep. Maybe he was mad that he was dying. Maybe he decided to strike out at Roy just out of spite."

"Ben, you can't keep opening up old wounds, stirring up pain. I hate to see it. It's just tearing you up," Kerry said, massaging his shoulders.

"But, what could it hurt if I just spent a little time investigating—you know, on my own. Sort of going over the evidence and seeing if it all adds up the way it seemed to at the trial. I remember reading about some college students in a law class who started investigating a murder as a project. The guy they were studying was on death row, just like Roy. You know what? They uncovered stuff that never came out at the trial—stuff the cops had completely overlooked. And they got the guy off! Turned out he was innocent just like he'd always said he was," Ben said.

"Ben, I love you more than anything in the whole world. I want to spend my life with you. So go on and do it. Do whatever you have to do. Whatever it takes to get this monkey off your back and bring you some peace—I'm behind you," Kerry said.

Ben turned to Kerry with a long look of love and gratitude. What a wonderful girl she was! Instead of ragging on him for messing up their date, she was supportive. He grabbed her and gave her a long kiss. Then he said, "You know, Kerry, Roy *did* have an alibi for the night the shooting happened."

"Yeah, I remember. His girlfriend said the two of them were together at her place all evening. But she was drunk that night, and she got all mixed up about the time. The prosecutor really made her look bad. Nobody in the courtroom believed her. The prosecutor convinced the jury that Roy could have left her for two hours and then come back. He strongly implied that she was so drunk she never would have noticed. You still keep up with her, Ben?"

"I've got her phone number, but I haven't talked to her since the trial. She really freaked out as the evidence against Roy started to build," Ben said.

"So go see her. Maybe it's time to talk to her again," Kerry said. "Maybe she'll remember something she didn't think to mention at the trial."

"Yeah, that's a good idea. I'll do that tomorrow. I feel awful about Noreen. After she testified she just sat there in the courtroom, sobbing like a kid," Ben remembered.

"Okay then. So as long as you have a plan, can we watch the movie now?" Kerry suggested.

"Okay," Ben said, putting his arm

around Kerry's shoulders and snuggling close to her.

After work the next day, Ben called Noreen Atwater. He was really nervous about what she would say. By now, Noreen probably had a new boyfriend. She probably wanted to forget that Roy Stephens had ever existed. After all, the whole thing had been an ugly, horrifying chapter in her life. If she refused to talk to Ben, he couldn't blame her for feeling that way.

But when Ben called, Noreen was very pleasant. "Hello, Ben," she said, sounding glad to hear from him. A baby was crying in the background. That worried Ben. Had Noreen gotten married and had a baby? All the more reason she wouldn't want to be bothered with bad old memories.

"How's everything going, Noreen?" Ben asked.

"Okay. Not *really* great, to tell you the truth—but okay, I guess," she said.

"Listen—would there be any chance of us getting together sometime? I need to talk to you," Ben said.

"Sure," Noreen said, "but what do you want to talk about?"

"Uh—I don't know how to say this without sounding like an idiot who won't face facts, Noreen. But I'm still not convinced that Roy really committed that murder," Ben said.

Noreen was silent for a moment. Then she said, "I'll be happy to talk to you, Ben—because I *know* he's innocent."

Hearing Noreen say that startled Ben. He felt a bolt of electricity go through his body. Up until now, his hope that Roy might be innocent had been like a frail, flickering flame in his heart. But Noreen's amazing statement had thrown gasoline on the flame and turned it into a roaring fire.

"So let's make a date, Ben. When should we meet?" Noreen asked.

"Is now a bad time?" Ben asked. It

was just about four in the afternoon.

"No, I guess now would be okay. Come on over. I'm at school a couple times a week, but I'm free this afternoon. I'm on welfare now—because of my son. I'm learning a lot about computers, though. Pretty soon I'll be qualified to get a good job," Noreen said.

Ben wrote down her address and quickly drove over to see her. He found Noreen's building in a rundown old neighborhood. Stucco was peeling from the walls of the buildings like sunburned skin. A dozen kids were playing in the gutters, and the weed-choked front yards were littered with broken toys. Groups of idle teenagers stood at graffiti-covered fences, staring out at a world that didn't seem to want them.

But the inside of Noreen's apartment was a very different story. The place was surprisingly well-kept. The second-hand furniture was decorated with ruffled covers and handmade pillows.

Everything looked shiny and spotless.

"Sit down," Noreen said. "I'll get us some coffee." She returned quickly with two steaming mugs. As Ben studied her face he noticed that tears were forming in her eyes.

"Oh, Ben, I still can't believe they convicted him," she cried out. "He was with *me*. He really was. But I was— well—I had a few drinks too many, and I was smashed. But I *know* for sure that he was here with me while the robbery was going on."

Ben nodded. "Yeah—you said that at the trial."

"But I failed him, Ben," Noreen groaned. "I failed Roy. If only I hadn't been drunk! If I could have remembered the details better, I might have convinced the jury. But that prosecutor just tore me apart. He made the jury believe that I was just a lying drunk trying to cover up for my murderer boyfriend!" Noreen wailed.

"No, no—don't blame yourself!" Ben said in a soft, comforting voice. "Roy brought this trouble on himself. He shouldn't have been hanging out with a loser like Pulver. The jury pegged Roy as a bum because of his record. If he hadn't been in trouble most of his life, they wouldn't have been so ready to believe the worst of him," Ben said.

Noreen reached out and touched Ben's arm. "But he was turning himself around, Ben—he really was. He'd learned to be a good plumber. We were gonna get married. We had a *future*, Ben!" Noreen said. Her desperate eyes seemed to beg for Ben's understanding.

"I believe you, Noreen. I could see that he was changing for the better," Ben said sadly. "If only there was some way to *prove* that Roy wasn't the one who did the shooting—"

Then the baby cried from the bedroom, and Noreen got up. "I've got to check on him," she said with a smile.

"The little guy probably wants to play. When he's done with his nap, he always wants to play."

"How old is he?" Ben asked.

"Thirteen months. Want to see him?" Noreen asked proudly.

"Sure," Ben said, following Noreen into the bedroom down the hall. The chubby wide-eyed baby stood in his playpen, gripping the railing.

"We were gonna be married in June," Noreen said in the saddest voice that Ben could ever remember hearing.

The shooting had happened in May.

"I never told Roy about the baby," Noreen said. "I know it would have just hurt him more—"

Ben stared at the child's face—at his brother's son!

Chapter 3

Ben's mind was spinning. Now he had another powerful reason to try to clear Roy Stephens. His brother had a child who would never know his father!

As he got ready to leave, Ben and Noreen walked to the door together. "I wish I could think of some way to help you . . . help *us*," Noreen said. "Have you talked to Larry Pulver's parents?"

"Pulver's parents?" Ben asked in surprise. "What good could that possibly do? And why would they be willing to talk to me? I can imagine the kind of people they are—you know, to have a son like him."

"No, Ben, that isn't fair. Sometimes good people have bad kids. I just remembered that they were with him when he died. Maybe he said something to them that he didn't tell the police. I know it's just a long shot, but . . ." Noreen said.

Ben didn't see any point in visiting the Pulvers. Just the thought of it sickened him. Larry Pulver was such a slimy character—a tall, rangy guy with sick, hateful eyes. In the last dozen years, he'd been arrested for armed robbery and for manslaughter. Both times he'd been let go. When Roy had started hanging out with Pulver at the bowling alley, Ben had been totally disgusted.

"How come you've taken up with that lowlife?" Ben had demanded of his brother.

"Because I'm a lowlife too," Roy had shot back. As usual, he never missed a chance to get in somebody's face. He *liked* to rebel. If his dad didn't like the color green, he'd go out and buy a green jacket. When he let his hair grow long and his dad said it looked good, he shaved his head bald. Ben could never figure it out—except for one thing. He suspected that Roy knew he wasn't as smart or as capable as his older brother. At some point along the way, he'd decided that he'd make his mark by being wild.

Ben got good grades in school. Roy was always close to flunking out. Ben was handsome and always got a lot of attention from the girls. Roy had less attractive features and was shy—so his social life wasn't as good. Ben had easily made the football team at Taft High. Roy had made only a halfhearted attempt, so he had failed to make the team.

Maybe he got so frustrated trying to be as good as Ben that he decided to quit trying. Maybe Roy finally found the one thing he could do better than Ben: He could raise more hell. He could be an all-star troublemaker. He could make Dad flush with rage in a wink, and turn the whole house upside down in a nanosecond. For his own reasons, Roy had played that card all the way to death row.

Checking the telephone book, Ben found the Pulvers' address and phone number. He still didn't know what good it would do to talk to them. Why should they want to help him? But he didn't have any better ideas, either.

Judging from the address, Ben guessed that Wilbur and Joyce Pulver must live in a nice neighborhood. Their house was in Holiday Hills, a big tract of Spanish-style homes in the rolling hills at the edge of town. It was hard to imagine a guy who looked and acted like Larry Pulver growing up in a place like that. Ben had expected the family to live above an empty pawn shop, a place with dirty, greasy windows.

Then it came to him that Noreen had been right. Good, solid people *do* have bad kids sometimes. Just like bad people sometimes have nice kids. There was no way to explain it.

Ben's own parents certainly didn't deserve a son like Roy. Even before he was convicted of murder he'd given them a ton of grief that they didn't have coming. They weren't *perfect* parents—but they were good people.

Ben sat drinking black coffee for about an hour, debating with himself about whether or not he should call the Pulver house. Then he finally made the call. He was still pretty sure it would do no good, but he had to give it a try.

Mr. Pulver answered the phone. He had a nice, polite baritone voice. He listened to Ben explain who he was and that he wanted to talk about appealing Roy Stephens' death sentence.

"I'm sorry. I can't see that talking to you would do either one of us any good," Mr. Pulver said.

"Still, I'd appreciate it if you'd let me come over and just have a few minutes with you and your wife," Ben said.

"Oh, no. That's entirely out of the question—about my wife, I mean. The poor woman has been very ill. I simply can't allow her to be bothered. We've been through enough, Mr. Stephens. As you very well know, young man, my wife and I buried a son under terrible circumstances," Mr. Pulver said.

"Please, Mr. Pulver! I think there's a good chance that my brother is innocent. If nobody does anything to stop it, he could be put to death. *Please*, Mr. Pulver! You wouldn't want an innocent man to die for something he didn't do, would you?" Ben pleaded.

"I sympathize with you, young man, I really do. But the truth is that our son and your brother were robbers. Your brother killed a clerk in that liquor store, and my son got killed. It was a horrible tragedy—for all of us. Our son paid with his life, and your brother must do the same. I'm afraid the tides of justice cannot be held back," Mr. Pulver said.

"Mr. Pulver, wouldn't *you* at least be willing to see me?" Ben asked. "Just you alone? We could meet somewhere—just the two of us."

"Mr. Stephens, my wife and I are seeking closure in this tragic situation. Listen to me—*I will not see you under any circumstances.* I absolutely refuse to be reminded of it. I'm sorry, but we're through talking now. Goodbye." And with that, he hung up.

Ben slumped sadly in his chair. He was surprised at how educated and intelligent Mr. Pulver had sounded. The guy spoke very well, and he seemed like a gentleman. Ben didn't hold his attitude against him. It must have been awful for the Pulvers to have a son like Larry— and then to have him die like that! No one could blame the man for wanting to close the door and put the whole disaster behind him.

But that left Ben staring at a brick

wall. He left his apartment and drove around aimlessly for an hour. For some reason he eventually ended up at the rundown bowling alley where Roy had met Pulver.

The bowling alley was in a sleazy, depressing neighborhood. All the telephone poles were decorated with work-at-home ads and political posters of elections long past. Many of the small stores around were empty and boarded up. Several homeless people slumped in doorways. Ben had been in the bowling alley only twice—both times looking for Roy. When Mom had tearfully pleaded with him to find Roy, Ben would search all of Roy's haunts—the bars, the video game arcades, the bowling alley.

When Ben finally found his brother, there would always be an ugly scene.

"Get off my case, Dudley Do-Right!" Roy would snarl.

But Ben was bigger and stronger. At first, he'd try to talk Roy into coming home—but then he'd have to drag him. Now Ben remembered one especially ugly confrontation. When Ben found him, Roy was playing video games with a tattooed guy in an orange windbreaker. Roy had already had too many beers, and he was showing off for his friend. He actually threw a roundhouse punch at Ben! Ben intercepted it, wrenched Roy's arm behind his back, and marched him out of the place while the tattooed guy laughed.

"I'll kill you for this!" Roy had threatened as Ben dragged him toward his truck.

"Shut up, you little punk!" Ben had barked at him. "Mom's worried sick. She called me in tears. You think I *like* having to go out at night and pull you out of one of these dives? I'm *tired* of it, you slimy little jerk! Why don't you get your act together?"

"Let me go!" Roy had howled as he

twisted and kicked at Ben.

"I'm getting you home, stupid—even if I have to hogtie you and tie you down in the back of my pickup," Ben said.

"I'll get you back for this!" Roy had screamed. "I swear I will!"

Ben had gotten his brother home that night—but by morning he was gone again. "Rescuing" him was hopeless. Roy was like a speeding car heading down a mountain without any brakes. If there was anything that could stop him, Ben didn't know what it could be.

Chapter 4

Ben walked around the area for 20 minutes or so, looking for Roy's old cronies. "One of those guys might know something," he thought to himself. All Ben needed was a crumb of information to hang onto and build on.

Then Ben spotted the tattooed guy. He looked the same as he had in the orange windbreaker, although he was wearing an old T-shirt tonight. Ben remembered that his name was Alex.

"Hey, you're Alex—right?" Ben called out to him.

"Yeah, yeah," the guy said, staring blankly at Ben. "Who're you?"

"I'm Ben Stephens. You knew my brother, Roy," Ben said.

"Oh, yeah, yeah! Hey, man, I'm sorry

about what happened. He got iced, didn't he?" Alex asked.

"No, he's still alive. But he was convicted of murder, and he's on death row," Ben said.

"Oh, yeah, that's right. It was the *other* guy who got shot," Alex said. "So ol' Roy's waiting for the long walk, huh? Must be some kinda ride to know that the end is coming."

"My brother hung out with you a lot, didn't he?" Ben asked, trying to sound casually interested.

"Yeah, me and Pulver and Roy—we were the three musketeers. And now, man, one's already dead and the other one is about to die. That leaves just me, right? Like, scary, huh? But then there was the kid, too. He ain't dead yet—so maybe there's a chance for me. I guess two outta four ain't such bad odds," Alex said, laughing nervously.

"The kid?" Ben asked. "Who was that? I don't think I ever met him."

"I never got his name. He'd come with Pulver. While we were drinking beer he'd always play the video games. Just a skinny kid. They all looked a lot alike, you know—Pulver, Roy, the kid— just skin and bones. I was the only fat one. When the four of us got together, Jake down at the taco stand, he'd say, "'Here comes three toothpicks and Porky.'" Alex laughed again.

"Alex, I think it's possible that my brother is innocent. I think that he *didn't* kill that guy. I'm looking for a way to reopen the case," Ben explained.

Alex frowned. "Nah, give it up, man, he's a dead duck. Once they get on death row they're as good as in their coffins. You think the DA and the cops are gonna spring a guy from death row after all the trouble they went to putting him there? In your dreams! Listen, these cops got their reps on the line."

"It's happened before, though," Ben pointed out. "Several men on death row have been released because someone found new evidence."

Alex shook his head. "Don't hold your breath until it happens, man."

Ben drove to the liquor store where the crime had taken place. It made him sick to walk in the place, but he had to. A pretty little Hispanic woman was behind the counter. She looked about 40.

"Good evening, ma'am. Have you worked here a long time?" Ben asked in a friendly voice.

The woman smiled and nodded. "Yeah, I been working here since my kids started school. Guess that's about five years now," she said.

Ben's heart raced. That meant she was working here when Carlos Oliver was murdered. On the night of the murder only Oliver had been in the store, but she'd been an employee then. Maybe she'd heard something that would be helpful.

Ben tried to hide his excitement.

"I bet you knew Carlos Oliver, huh?" he asked casually.

The woman's smile quickly faded. In a tight little voice she said, "Oh, he's dead. Seems like a long time now."

"Yeah, I heard about that. A real tragedy—a great kid like that. His whole life ahead of him. Must have really upset everybody around here," Ben said.

The woman looked surprised, and then she frowned. "Nobody liked Carlos. I mean, it's too bad he was killed and all that, but—" She shuddered, shaking her head. "He was a bad one—*muy malo*."

Chapter 5

Ben was startled, to say the least. At the trial, Carlos Oliver had been portrayed as an upstanding young man, a model son, a promising student.

"*Muy malo?*" Ben repeated. He knew only a little Spanish. But he did know that those two words meant *very bad*.

"Yes, he was not nice—with girls," the woman said.

"What do you mean?" Ben pressed her. Maybe there was something here. He wasn't sure what it was, but maybe there was a bit of information that would lead somewhere else. When you had nothing to go on, every scrap of information could be important.

The woman looked around to make sure no one else was in earshot. Then

THE CASE OF THE DEAD DUCK

she went on. "He pushed his attentions on girls who maybe did not want it. He tried to date my sister. She said 'no,' but he kept on hounding her. One time he tried to put a drug in her soda so he could mess with her and she couldn't stop him. After a while he started dating another girl. I saw him being very rough with her one time. He shoved her in his car and she hit her head on the door. When the cut bled, he cursed her. I always thought that might be the reason he was killed. Like maybe somebody got mad and wouldn't take what he was doing to their daughter or their sister anymore."

"No," Ben said, remembering the testimony at the trial. "He was killed by robbers. That came out in court. There was fifty dollars in the till."

The woman sneered. "No way. Even robbers are not so stupid. Everybody in this neighborhood knows what the slow nights are. There was nothing worth robbing in the till. A robber from around here would have known it wasn't worth hitting the store that night. Anyway—the guy next door in the billiards place said he heard yelling and fighting before the shooting," she said.

"I remember. The billiards guy testified at the trial. But he thought the robbers were probably just yelling for the money—" Ben said.

"No way. I think it was a *grudge*," the woman said. "I think those guys came in the store with just one thing in mind—to beat up or kill Carlos Oliver. I think Carlos went too far—hurt some girl, you know—and he got killed over that," the woman said confidently.

"Did you ever tell the police about your suspicion?" Ben asked.

"No. Nobody ever talked to me," the woman said.

Not even Roy's lawyer, Ben thought grimly. The Stephenses were not rich people. That's why Roy had been

45

assigned a public defender. Ben supposed that the guy had tried his best. But he surely didn't have the time or the money to do a first-rate investigation.

Ben left the liquor store wondering if maybe Pulver had a sister—a girl who'd been abused by Carlos Oliver. It could be that he and some other guy went there to settle the score.

But why would Pulver have insisted to his dying breath that it was a robbery? Why would he say that Roy Stephens had fired the fatal shot that killed Oliver? If the whole thing had been a grudge fight—why wouldn't Pulver have admitted what happened?

Chapter 6

Ben felt confused and weary. He shook his head as he drove off, wondering what to do next. He *was* coming up with all kinds of new jigsaw puzzle pieces. But he had no idea where they fit in. He had absolutely nothing yet that would make the DA even talk to him about reopening the case. But at least he had come up with some new theories—whether they eventually turned out to be true or not.

Roy had sworn that he wasn't with Pulver that night. If that was the case, who *was* there? Not only Pulver but also Oliver had identified Roy as the shooter. But maybe the guy who really shot Oliver just *looked* like Roy. Maybe Oliver glanced at the snapshot quickly and *accidentally* made the wrong ID.

What was it that Alex had said? *They all looked alike, you know—Pulver, Roy, the kid.* . . . They were all about the same size, very thin, and dark. At least Pulver and Roy were. Ben didn't know who the kid was or what he looked like.

The kid. Who the devil was the kid?

All of a sudden Ben was desperate to find out. Then it came to him in a flash that the kid might be the key. Where was the kid?

Ben returned to the bar next to the bowling alley. This time he found Alex drinking with some of his buddies.

"Have you got a minute, Alex? I gotta ask you about something. Do you happen to know if Larry Pulver had a sister?" Ben asked.

Alex shrugged. "Dunno. He never talked to me about no family. He was on the outs with his folks. He never talked about personal stuff. I never even knew if he had a babe," he said.

Ben walked out of the bar, frustrated. Then he grabbed his cell phone and called the Pulver house. He was shaking with nervousness, but he had to at least give it a try.

Mr. Pulver answered, "Yes?"

"Is your daughter home?" Ben asked.

"Who's this?" Mr. Pulver demanded.

"A friend from high school. I just got back in town, and I thought the two of us might get together," Ben said in a friendly voice.

"Well, son, Angie doesn't live here anymore. She's got her own place now. What's your name, anyway?" Mr. Pulver asked curiously.

"This is Artie Thompson," Ben said, plucking the name from his imagination. "Angie and I were in history class together our senior year."

"Oh, you went to Emerson High?" Mr. Pulver asked.

"Yeah, that's right," Ben said eagerly.

"Well, I don't recall hearing your

name—but Angie had lots of friends, of course. Would you like her phone number?" Mr. Pulver said.

"That'd be great," Ben said. "We worked on our senior project together. Lucky for me that she was so smart. I'd just like to see her and talk over old times. You know, maybe get together for coffee if she'd like."

"She goes to CSUN now," Mr. Pulver said with a touch of pride.

"Hey, how about that? I'm enrolling there next semester," Ben said, surprising himself at what a good liar he was.

When Ben got off the phone he thought about the best way to contact Angie Pulver. With her, he couldn't pretend that he was an old classmate. She would know there had never been an Artie Thompson. But, Ben thought, he could always say that he was an old friend of her brother's. That story might fly. Yeah, that would work! He could say that he and Larry had been close a few years back. That might get his foot in the door. Unless, of course, she hated Larry for being such a creep—like Ben's dad hated Roy.

But it was Ben's only chance.

Chapter 7

The phone in Angie's apartment rang several times before she answered. "Hello?"

"Angie Pulver?" Ben asked.

"Yeah, who's this?"

"Artie Thompson," Ben said. He'd decided it was too risky to use his last name. She might recognize it as the name of the guy who robbed the liquor store with her brother that fateful night.

"We haven't met, but I knew your brother Larry a couple of years ago. We even roomed together briefly. He left some personal stuff with me when he moved out. I just got back in town and heard the bad news. I wanted to tell you how sorry I was—and to give the stuff back to somebody in his family. Larry mentioned that he had a younger sister—and I guess that's you."

For a minute or so, Angie didn't say a word. Then her voice was careful. "What *kind* of stuff?" she asked.

"Photos. Family photos. I didn't want to just toss them out. I know how precious family pictures can be— especially, you know, when there's been a death," Ben said. Eventually he would have to admit to her that all this was a lie, a sneaky ploy to trick her into talking to him. But that wasn't important now. Just getting to meet her was the important thing. Because getting Roy off death row was all that mattered.

"Yes, well, I'd like to have them, of course," she said. "I'm over at Cal State Northridge, you know. There's a little hamburger place across the street, down a few blocks from the library. Hal's Hamburgers. Could you meet me there?"

"Sure," Ben said. "When?"

"Would tomorrow morning around

9:30 be okay?" Angie said.

"That would be great," Ben said. He'd call the real estate office and tell them he was going to be in a little late. He'd say he had to take care of pressing family business. They'd understand.

Ben went early to Hal's Hamburgers to wait for Angie. What did she look like? He might have seen her at Roy's trial—if she had come at all. He didn't think so. He could remember only Mr. and Mrs. Pulver.

At exactly 9:30 a very pretty girl came in the door, looking around.

"Over here, Angie!" Ben called out as he waved to her.

She came over and sat in the booth across from Ben. He noticed that she had a sad, haunted look in her eyes. "Were you and Larry close?" she asked.

"Nah, not really. We just bowled together a few times. Then we rented this place together—but he moved on before we got to be really tight," Ben said.

Tears filled the girl's eyes and she dabbed at them with a handkerchief. "Larry got into a lot of trouble all the time," she said. "The truth is that he wasn't a good person. I'm not going to pretend that he was. But there wasn't a brother in the whole world who took better care of his sister—I'll give him that." She paused then and gave Ben a questioning look. "So, where are the pictures?" she asked.

"Angie," Ben asked suddenly, "did you ever date Carlos Oliver?"

Angie Pulver gasped. She came close to knocking over her cup of coffee as her hand shot to her mouth.

"Who told you that?" She demanded.

"It's true, isn't it? You dated him and he treated you badly. That's why your brother was in the liquor store that night, wasn't it? It didn't have anything to do with robbery. Larry went there to deal with the guy who messed with his sister," Ben said. He was talking fast, trying to catch Angie off guard so she might blurt out the truth. Instead, Angie stood up, her thin face filled with hurt and anger.

"*Who are you?* You tricked me, didn't you? You aren't any friend of Larry's. What do you want?" she cried.

"Angie, yeah—you're right. I lied and I tricked you. I'm sorry. My name is Ben Stephens, and my kid brother is sitting on death row. I think he's innocent. That's why I'm desperately trying to find out the truth about that liquor store killing. I want to save my brother's life if I can. Listen, Angie—my brother has a baby son he'll never know. And he's got parents who are sick with grief and despair—" Ben rattled on.

The girl looked wild. She shook her head in disbelief. "I don't want to talk to you. I'm getting out of here. Our family has suffered enough over this. Larry and your brother were robbers—and that's all there was to it! I'm not letting my family get dragged through this whole thing again. My mother is sick. In fact my mother's health is so bad that she stays in bed most of the time. She can't go anywhere or do anything. This has just *ruined* her life! So go away and leave us alone!" Angie turned and ran for the door.

"Wait, Angie! Tell me the truth. Was Larry in that liquor store to pay Carlos Oliver back for hurting you? The truth could save my brother's life, Angie. You've got to tell me if it was a fight over something instead of a robbery. Please help me! Roy's death sentence might be commuted—even if he was there," Ben shouted.

Angie stared at Ben in horror. "Get away from me!" she cried.

"Think about it, Angie! Do you want an innocent man to die because of something you know to be a lie?" Ben shouted after the fleeing girl. But she ran down the sidewalk and he didn't follow her anymore. A couple of college guys who looked like football linemen saw Angie run away from him. Now they stared at Ben in a hostile way. They probably thought Ben was just another jerk harassing a girl. It was clear that they were about to intervene.

Ben watched the girl disappear into a crowd of students on the sidewalk. His hands clenched in frustration. He was onto something—he *knew* it. But if Angie refused to tell the truth, he was up against a brick wall.

After work that day, Ben went over to Kerry Underwood's apartment and told her everything.

"Why are the Pulvers stonewalling?" Ben asked. "Their son is dead. He can't be hurt anymore. Would they rather he be remembered as a robber in a fatal stickup or as a brother defending his sister? It doesn't make sense. It seems like they *want* my brother to die in the gas chamber, Kerry!"

When Ben came in Kerry had been washing her hair, and now she was toweling it dry. "But why did Larry Pulver tell the police it was a robbery while he was dying? The man was *dying*, Ben—it doesn't make sense that he wouldn't tell the truth," she said.

Ben stared at her. "So what are you saying?" he asked.

Kerry wrapped her clean wet hair in a towel and said, "I don't know. Maybe the Pulvers are protecting somebody else. Maybe they don't want it known that Angie ever had a relationship with Oliver. If this Oliver guy really was a sordid creep—it could certainly be that they're trying to protect their daughter's reputation."

"So my poor brother should die in the gas chamber to protect little Angie Pulver's good name?" Ben demanded.

"Hold on, Ben! I'm not saying that what they're doing is *right*," Kerry said. "I could be way off base about the whole thing. But listen, Ben. I just got a wild idea. There may be something else you could check out—"

"Give it to me, babe," Ben said. "I'm desperate!"

Chapter 8

"What do you think of this, Ben?" Kerry said thoughtfully. "Maybe the Pulvers *aren't* trying to protect Angie's reputation. Maybe they're protecting the guy who really *did* pull the trigger on Carlos Oliver."

"The *kid*!" Ben cried out. "Yeah, that might be it. There was another guy who hung out with Pulver. Alex, the tattooed guy, called him *the kid*. Alex even said the kid looked like Roy. *Yeah!* Maybe Oliver identified Roy, thinking he was the kid. It could have been an honest mistake. Or how about this—maybe Pulver deliberately nailed Roy to get the heat off the kid!"

"Ben," Kerry said, "did you ever wonder if the Pulvers might have *another* son? That would make sense, too, wouldn't it? Doesn't it seem possible that the Pulvers might be trying to protect another son?"

Ben was back at CSUN the next morning, waiting for Angie Pulver. He didn't care if she wanted to see him or not. He *had* to know if she had a brother who might have been the second guy in the liquor store that night.

Ben finally found Angie walking along with a book under her arm. He called out to her, "Angie—you have another brother, don't you? Was your brother the other guy with Larry that night in the liquor store?"

Angie let out a cry of anguish. She clutched her book and screamed, "Leave me alone! I don't have another brother! Just leave me alone!"

"Tell me the truth, Angie. Don't let an innocent man die for something he didn't do. Angie, listen! It wouldn't be so bad if Larry and your other brother started that fight to protect you from Carlos Oliver. They wouldn't come down too hard on your brother. It'd be just second-degree murder—or even manslaughter! Remember that Carlos had a gun, too. But for my brother it's death row. Please, Angie! They're gonna kill my brother!" Ben yelled.

"Stay away from me, or I'll call security!" Angie cried as she turned away.

Two guys came up to Ben then. One of them appeared to be Angie's friend.

"Go on to class, Angie," the big guy said. "We'll handle this crazy dude."

The guys grabbed Ben, one on each arm, and hustled him down the street and behind the math building.

"What's your problem, man?" one of the guys snarled.

"That girl knows the truth about a murder that an innocent man is going to die for," Ben said. "The guy is my brother. I'm trying to save my brother."

Both guys laughed out loud. "What've you been smoking, dude?" one of them asked in a sarcastic voice. The bigger of the pair sneered.

"It's true," Ben insisted. "My brother is on death row. He's gonna die unless that girl tells what she knows." He knew it all sounded crazy and hysterical, but he didn't know how else to say it.

"You got mental problems, man," one of the guys snorted.

"Yeah," the other one agreed. "Listen, dude—you go back to whatever halfway house you've been sent to. Take your medicine, and leave Angie alone. If we see you coming around here hassling that girl again, you'll be sorry. Do you know what's going to happen? We're gonna dump you head first into one of those garbage dumpsters until you're choking on dirty hot dog wrappers—understand?"

Chapter 9

Right after work, Ben went down to the County Hall of Records. He hoped the Pulvers had lived in the area for a long time. Then it would be easy to find the birth records of all their children.

Ben found Lawrence Edgar Pulver's birth notice on film. The guy had been 29 when he died. Then Ben found Angela Marie Pulver's birth certificate. She was now 21. A few minutes later, his heart pounding, Ben came across the third child born to the Pulvers!

Kirk David Pulver was several years younger than Angie. He'd have been just 16 at the time of the shooting.

No doubt he was "the kid." Ben felt sure of it. Larry and Kirk had gone to the liquor store to take on Carlos Oliver for something he had done to their sister. Kirk must be the one who had done the shooting. That would explain everything: To protect his kid brother, Larry Pulver had decided to throw his buddy, Roy Stephens, to the wolves!

Ben's pulse was racing. He thought he had it all figured out—but he had no *proof*. So far it was all theory. Unless Angie was willing to tell the truth, he didn't have enough to help Roy.

Ben called Roy's lawyer, Mr. Blaine, and told him everything. The lawyer listened politely and then said, "Look, Ben, don't get too excited. None of this is proven fact. You're just speculating. You don't have a shred of proof that any of this even happened.

"Carlos Oliver might never have laid eyes on Angela Pulver. The brother, Kirk, could be a nerdy little college guy who never handled a gun in his life. All we have is the sworn word of Pulver and the victim, Oliver. And they both said that Roy Stephens was the shooter. But still—what you've told me should be enough to at least get another appeal underway. Clearly, the jury should have been told about any relationship between the victim and the culprits."

Ben burst out in frustration, "Mr. Blaine, Angie has *got* to tell the truth! I've talked to the girl myself. She's not a monster. But how can she live with herself, knowing that her silence has condemned an innocent man?"

"She might feel very strongly about protecting her own family," Mr. Blaine said. "Think about it, Ben. Perhaps she *did* have a relationship with Carlos Oliver. Let's say she feels guilty that her poor choice of friends caused her brother to die. I'll tell you what, Ben: I'll contact her. I'll explain it all in detail. If in fact her 16-year-old brother did the shooting, he wouldn't be facing serious prison time. He was just a kid at the time. I'll assure her that a very good case could be made for self-defense."

Ben thanked the lawyer and put down the phone. He was glad that Mr. Blaine was taking action. But he couldn't wait for the wheels of justice to grind along at such a slow pace. Somehow he had to make Angie Pulver realize what her silence was doing. Even if he had to risk getting roughed up by her buddies on the football squad.

Ben's brother was sitting on death row. Mom was in deep depression, taking pills to sleep and pills to wake up. Ben had watched his 45-year-old mother go from a vibrant woman who looked years younger than she was, to an old woman—a *joyless* old woman who never went shopping anymore, never had lunch with her girlfriends.

And Ben's dad had changed from a happy, contented man into a bitter workaholic. All during Ben's growing up years, he had admired his parents' wonderful relationship. And now even that had turned sour. They didn't go to Vegas anymore; they didn't go fishing on the Colorado River. Now they just barely existed in their own little worlds within the same house—each of them grieving for Roy in their own way.

In a burst of enthusiasm, Ben decided to find out where Angie lived and try to confront her there. But then he changed his mind. He was pretty sure that would be too threatening to her. He had to confront her at the college. Somehow he had to hit just the right chord to motivate her to cooperate.

Ben drove to CSUN the next morning and looked around for Angie. He stood hidden behind some shrubbery until she was very close, and then he stepped out into her path. He knew what she would do if she saw him from a distance. She'd run off in a different direction, even if it meant missing class.

"Angie!" he cried in an impassioned voice. "I'm *begging* you to listen to me.

I don't want to harass you, but I'm fighting for my brother's life!"

Angie clutched her book to her chest, her face a mask of anguish. "P-please go away," she whimpered. "I can't help you! Just go away!"

"Angie, your kid brother shot Carlos Oliver because of something the guy did to you: I know that in my gut. When the truth comes out, they probably won't even send your brother to jail—but my brother is gonna die!" Ben cried.

"I—I can't help it," Angie said, crying softly, the tears running down her cheeks. "It's too late!" She didn't deny the truth of what Ben was saying. She didn't deny a word of it.

"Angie, I'm counting on you to do the right thing. This situation is tearing my family apart. It's just not right that an innocent man should die for something he never did. He wasn't even *there* that night!" Ben said.

Angie Pulver was shaking. She wiped

the tears off her face with the back of her hand. *"I c-can't!"* she cried. "They did it for *me.* Like a fool, I went out with Carlos, and he put something in my drink. Then he—he—did what he wanted to me. Larry and Kirk went over there fighting mad. Kirk was wild then. In those days, he hung out with Larry. But since then he's become an honor student in college. He's a wonderful kid! After what he did for me, I can't betray Kirk. He's building a good life now."

"Yeah, but he's building his good life on my brother's grave, Angie," Ben said bitterly.

Ben never saw the two big guys coming until they were right on top of him. Apparently they'd been shadowing Angie, watching out for her. Just as they had warned him, they were making it their business to prevent Ben from harassing her. Now one of them roughly grabbed Ben's shoulder and swung him around.

"We warned you, dude!" the bigger man shouted. "Whatever your beef was, we told you to leave the girl alone, or you'd have us to deal with!"

"You asked for this, man," the other guy said, rubbing his hands together.

One of the guys drove a fist into Ben's midsection, dropping him to his knees. Before he could scramble up, Ben caught another blow to the face and tumbled over backward. Now he could taste blood and feel it streaming down his face from a cut on his forehead.

Ben struggled to get to his feet, but a heavy shoe found his left ribs. He heard bones crack. Then everything got hazy. Ben was in a world of pain. He couldn't get up, or hardly even move. Again he felt blows and kicks raining down on him. He tried curling up in a ball to defend his body, but even that didn't help.

Then, from somewhere, Ben heard a long, drawn-out scream. It was like the wild cry of a dying animal in the wilderness. He knew it didn't come from his own throat. His mouth was swollen and bloody, and he couldn't even speak. The scream went on and on like a siren, but Ben couldn't tell what it was. He was so dizzy and dazed that he didn't even care.

Finally the scream seemed to fade away. Ben lay in the dirt, not conscious of anything. He couldn't hear or see— and if they were still kicking him, he couldn't feel it.

But the scream had continued, even though Ben could no longer hear it. It was the wail of a siren.

Now people were running to the spot where Ben lay. Somebody called 911, and the police and the paramedics drove up. By then, of course, Angie's two "bodyguards" were long gone. None of the bystanders seemed willing to give the cops any names. Most of the students seemed to think it was none of their business. The bloodied guy on the ground must have done something awfully bad to deserve such a beating.

Ben didn't remember a thing about the paramedics giving him first aid. He didn't remember being loaded into the ambulance or the drive to the hospital emergency room.

Ben didn't hear his parents arrive— or Kerry, or Mr. Blaine, the lawyer. But they were all there, either pacing in the waiting room or standing at his bedside in the ER.

When Ben woke up, the ER nurse looked down at him and said, "You took a bad beating, young man—but you'll be okay. Your X-rays showed some busted ribs, and you'll be staying here overnight for observation. The doctor will come back in about 30 minutes to talk to you."

Ben's mother and Kerry were at his bedside. He painfully turned his head to talk to his mother. "Mom, I'm sorry you got dragged down here."

Mrs. Stephens smiled. Ben was amazed—she looked younger than she had looked in a long time. "It's all right, darling," she said. "Mr. Blaine just took a statement from Angela Pulver. I can't believe it, Ben. What she said exonerates Roy—"

Kerry took Ben's hand. "Seeing you getting beaten to a pulp turned out to be too much for Angie," she said softly. "At first she couldn't stop screaming. But when the cops got there she *demanded* to make a statement. Can you believe it? She said she needed to tell the truth about an old murder case," Kerry said.

"It's a miracle, Ben! They think Roy might be coming home before too long!" Mom said in a shaky voice. "And we owe it all to you!"

Ben smiled—even though it split his swollen lip and made it bleed. He didn't care. He smiled anyway because he couldn't help it. *At last* there was something to smile about.

COMPREHENSION QUESTIONS

IDENTIFYING CHARACTERS

1. Which character knew for sure that Roy Stephens was innocent?

2. Which character finally told the truth about who killed the liquor store clerk?

3. Which character didn't know that he had a son?

VOCABULARY

1. Ben's "personable" qualities made him a more successful real estate agent. What does *personable* mean?

2. The liquor store clerk was "mortally" wounded. What does *mortally* mean? Explain your thinking.

3. Kerry Underwood suspected that Carlos Oliver was a "sordid" creep. What does *sordid* mean?